The Dream Child

DAVID McPHAIL

The Dream Child

E. P. DUTTON   NEW YORK

for Duane—Isn't everything just a dream
after all?
and
for Emilie, with love

Unicorn is a registered trademark of E. P. Dutton
Library of Congress number 84-18755
ISBN 0-525-44366-5
Published in the United States by E. P. Dutton,
2 Park Avenue, New York, N.Y. 10016,
a division of NAL Penguin Inc.
Published simultaneously in Canada by
Fitzhenry and Whiteside Limited, Toronto
Editor: Ann Durell   Designer: Riki Levinson
Printed in Hong Kong by South China Printing Co.
First Unicorn Edition 1988   COBE
10 9 8 7 6 5 4 3 2 1

As the day follows the sun
    into tonight,
down from the endless sky
    and beyond
comes the Dream Child
    with
    Tame Bear beside her.

The Dream Child
    is sleeping
and the cows and the sheep
    keep watch,
    for
    even Tame Bear
    is still too sleepy
    to keep
        his
            eyes
                open.

Then as the moon rises,
its warm breath hanging
    in the
    chilly air,
the Dream Child
    awakes,
    nudges Tame Bear,
    and together
in a boat with wings
    they sail

to where
    the frogs are singing
            loudly
    and keeping the chickens
            awake.
''We need to roost!''
  the weary hens
    tell the Dream Child—
so she teaches
    the frogs
    to hum
    soft roosting songs.

The roar of a hungry lion
   comes riding
   on the wind.
The Dream Child
   and
   Tame Bear
bring him
   baskets of fruit
   and
   canned hams
and carry him
   about
until he is strong enough
   to hunt
   again.

Tame Bear is homesick,
so he
and the Dream Child
    return
    to the Bear Place
where Tame Bear's mother
    is Queen.

She hugs
    them both
and licks them
    with
    her great
    honey-coated
    tongue.

Soon
　the time
comes
　to leave
the Bear Place
　and
　fly to
the deepest darkest
part of the
　forest,
where
　the moon
never shines
and where
　the Giants
who live there
never smile
　and
are always
　angry.

But when
the Dream Child
    and
    Tame Bear
pull apart
    the treetops,
the moon
    shines
        down
            and
like a golden key
    unlocks
    the hearts
of the Giants,
    and
they smile
    and
are happy.

A giraffe,
come to sip the
    evening's coolness,
is stuck
    fast
in the mud
    of the
swamp,
where every
    creeping
    crawling
    thing
is trying
to outstare
the other.

And
in the pale
reflected
  light
of
  all those
  eyes,
the Dream Child
  and Tame Bear
pull
  the giraffe
  free
and wave
  good-bye.
For a brighter star
  beckons.

It is a great fire
around which
    dances
a family
    of apes
all squeezed
    together.
But the apes
    make room
    for
Tame Bear
    and
the Dream Child
    and call them
Friends.

The dance
goes on
    and on
until
    Tame Bear
      and
the Dream Child
    are too weary
    to stand.
Then
    in the glow
of the fire's
    dying embers,
the apes
    carry them
to their waiting boat.

And as the night
    follows the
    moon
    into yesterday,
the Dream Child
    and
    Tame Bear
    curl up
        in
the bottom of the boat
and drift
through
    the
        endless sky

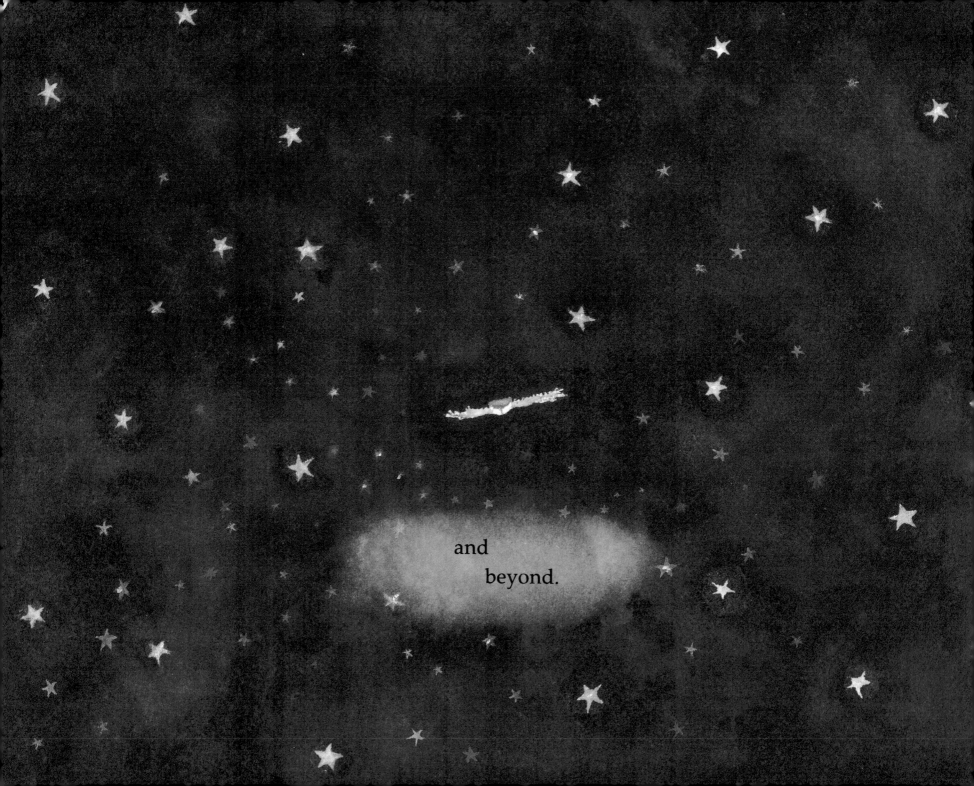

and
beyond.